THE AMAZING AGE OF
DINOSAURS

Written and Illustrated by Fred Wierum
Printed by CreateSpace, An Amazon.com Company

Dinosaurs were the most amazing creatures to have ever lived, yet all we have left of them are the bones they left behind.

Even though these beasts are gone, we still love them today.

Everyone loves Dinosaurs, especially the little ones!

Thanks to new discoveries and careful studying, we know a lot about our favorite Dinosaurs!

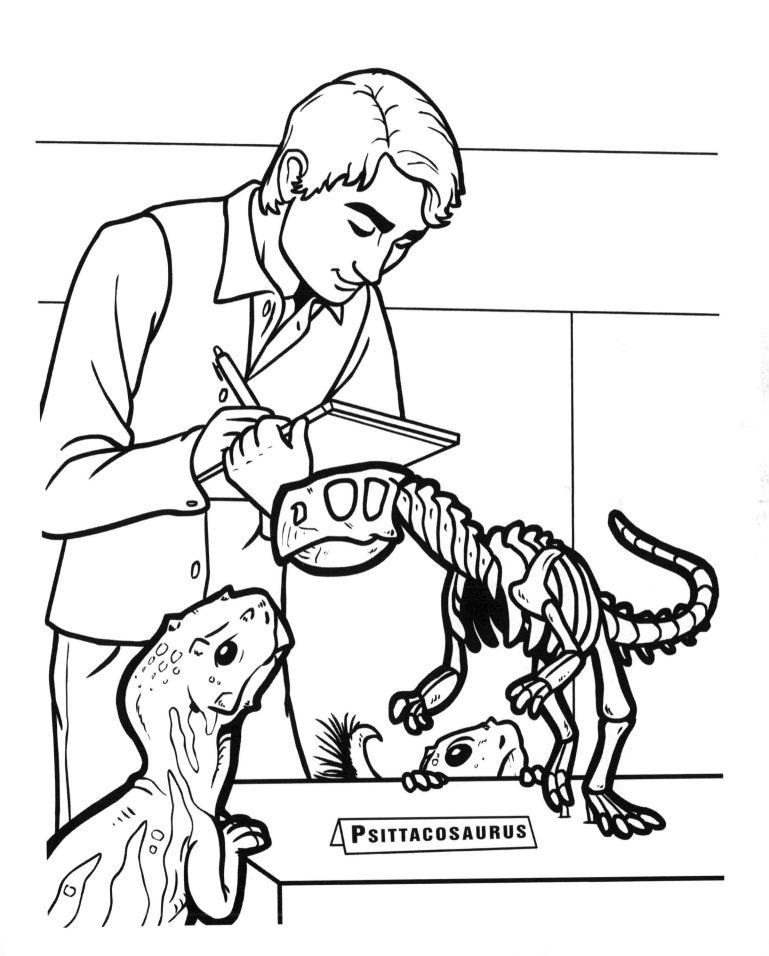

PSITTACOSAURUS

The age of Dinosaurs began over 200 million years ago. The earth was much warmer back then.

The first Dinosaurs appeared here in the Triassic period, like Coelophysis. Coelophysis was an early ancestor of meat-eating dinosaurs.

Coelophysis lived with Plateosaurus. They were tall dinosaurs.

Plateosaurus ate plants and was the ancestor of all the long-necked dinosaurs.

FINISH THE PICTURE:

Complete the trees so the Plateosaurus can eat his fill!

Plateosaurs love their greens!

Plant-eaters like Plateosaurus had to be careful from meat-eaters like Liliensternus.

Liliensternus was a bigger meat-eater than Coelophysis. It had two small crests on its head.

But Liliensternus wasn't the biggest meat-eater. Postosuchus was the biggest bad boy of his time!

Postosuchus wasn't a dinosaur. He was a relative of crocodiles and alligators.

A long with Postosuchus, there also lived another relative of crocodiles.

Desmatosuchus was a herbivore that had large spikes on its sides. It had a shovel-like nose, like a pig.

MAZE:

Help the early Dinosaurs make it through the
Triassic period to the
Jurassic period.

Dilophosaurus was a large meat-eating dinosaur from the early Jurassic period. He had two big crests on his head.

Like Liliensternus, Dilophosaurus preyed upon dinosaurs like
Anchisaurus, another relative of long-necked dinosaurs.

Baraposaurus was one of the first true long-necked dinosaurs. They lived in what is now India.

Scelidosaurus also lived in the early Jurassic. He was the ancestor of the armored dinosaurs.

Cryolophosaurus was a big meat-eater that lived in Antarctica. He had a strange crest over his head.

The late Jurassic period saw dinosaurs spread all over the world. Small herbivores like Dryosaurus were common.

Dryosaurus was a really fast plant-eating dinosaur. It was like the Gazelle of the Jurassic.

As fast as Dryosaurus was, he could still not escape the jaws of big carnivores like Ceratosaurus.

Ceratosaurus was a medium sized meat-eater. He had three large horns on his head that made him look very fierce!

WHICH IS DIFFERENT:
Three Ceratosaurs are the same.
Can you find the one that is different?

A)

B)

C)

D)

Some Ceratosaurus skulls have been found with teeth that grew so long they went pass the bottom jaw!

One of the most famous dinosaurs alive at the time was our old favorite, Stegosaurus.

This dinosaur had a double row of boney plates running down its back with 4 spikes on its tail.

Stegosaurus might have used his plates for showing off to other Stegosaurs.

He most likely used his tail for defense from predators like Ceratosaurus.

One of Stegosaurus' neighbors was Camptosaurus, a larger plant-eater related to Dryosaurus.

Camptosaurus was about 16 feet long and had a small spike on its thumb.

MAZE:

Show the migrating Camptosaurus the way to the feeding grounds, but be careful of predators!

One species of Camptosaurus had a short skull and may have been kind of cute.

The largest creatures that ever walked the earth appeared in the Jurassic. These types of dinosaurs are called Sauropods.

Giant behemoths like Apatosaurus stomped their way through the land,
eating up to 5 tons of vegetation.

Apatosaurus was originally called Brontosaurus because it was thought the bones of both dinosaurs were the same animal.

But recent studies show that Brontosaurus was actually real and its own dinosaur. Brontosaurus has returned!

Another big sauropod that lived with Apatosaurus was the tall Brachiosaurs. They were rarer than other sauropods.

Brachiosaurus was so tall he could look through a window three stories high! That's over 35 feet!

Brachiosaurus was so big it didn't have to worry about sneaky predators like Allosaurus. But baby Brachiosaurus were in constant danger.

Allosaurus was the top predator of the Jurassic and may be the biggest.
He had big arms for a large theropod and 2 crests in front of his eyes.

We're not certain but Allosaurus hunting in groups could be a possibility.

Evidence suggests that Allosaurus and Stegosaurus were common enemies. Maybe Stegosaurus was Allosaurus' favorite food.

Far, far away, in Jurassic Europe, another theropod hunted for food, but this little dinosaur doesn't run after its food. It used its wings!

This is Archaeopteryx, one of the first winged dinosaurs. The name Archaeopteryx means "original bird".

Archaeopteryx lived alongside its relative, Compsognathus. Compsognathus was a small 4 foot long carnivore that was covered in downy feathers.

Scientists found stomach contents of
Compsognathus and it turns out they were frequent lizard eaters.

MATCH:

Can you remember each Dinosaur's name from the Jurassic? See if you can match each name to the correct dinosaur without looking back.

Apatosaurus

Coelophysis

Stegosaurus

Allosaurus

Brachiosaurus

At the end of the Jurassic, many dinosaurs went extinct. Paleontologists don't know why, but new dinosaurs came in their place.

The Cretaceous period brought new dinosaurs of many different, interesting, and truly bizarre shapes and sizes. Many of which came from small beginnings, like the feathered Guanlong.

Guanlong was the early ancestor of T. Rex and his relatives. They originated from what is now known as China.

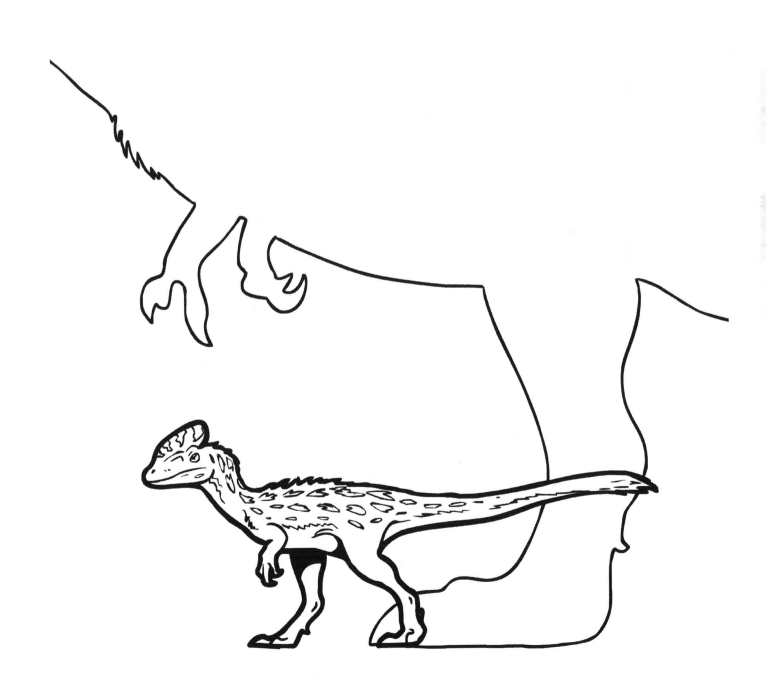

More famous predators appeared in the Cretaceous, like the raptors! Utahraptor is the largest and one of the first raptor dinosaurs.

Utahraptor was 24 feet long and 6 feet high. Not only that, but the sickle claws on their third toes were probably 15 inches long!

Utahraptor lived with and hunted other dinosaurs in the area, like Gastonia. Gastonia was an armored dinosaur related to Ankylosaurus.

Gastonia was a herbivore and had rows of big, pointy spikes along its sides for protection from predators like Utahraptor.

One of the most successful Dinosaurs was the Iguanodon. These big herbivores lived on every continent and lasted 75 million years on earth.

Iguanodon is famous for having a large thumb spike on its hands. Experts don't know what it was for exactly but it may have been used to defend itself.

WORD SEARCH:
Find and circle the names and words in the puzzle below.

```
G  S  H  W  U  P  V  F  V  B  R  S  E  S  B
U  T  A  H  R  A  P  T  O  R  Z  M  R  P  I
U  V  H  L  A  N  P  I  S  Z  W  S  E  V
Z  L  P  T  L  E  R  O  V  I  B  R  E  H  F
F  B  J  H  O  O  P  S  D  Z  K  Z  K  B  U
O  D  D  E  W  N  S  N  R  E  F  T  I  M  C
A  K  I  R  R  T  O  A  Z  J  X  Y  P  R  E
D  K  N  O  D  O  N  A  U  G  I  B  S  U  B
Q  O  O  P  G  L  V  G  P  R  L  O  N  H  A
Y  C  S  O  S  O  R  I  K  S  U  A  F  O  J
B  N  A  D  T  G  V  Y  N  M  I  S  U  B  E
H  E  U  K  C  I  B  N  U  R  Z  N  V  S  P
S  U  R  U  A  S  O  T  A  P  A  N  Q  J  X
F  C  Q  K  B  T  R  S  W  V  X  C  S  F  Z
F  S  O  E  K  X  Q  D  D  B  N  U  O  E  L
K  L  M  A  L  J  R  M  E  K  J  K  U  Q  Q
```

Allosaurus	Apatosaurus	Carnivore
Dinosaur	Ferns	Herbivore
Iguanodon	Paleontologist	Size
Spikes	Theropod	Utahraptor

Another way to use his thumb spike would be to help it forage for food, either to dig up roots or pull down branches.

One of Iguanodon's neighbors is the fierce Neovenator. This 25 foot long carnivore roamed prehistoric Europe and was probably the reason Iguanodon needed defense.

The fish-eating Baryonyx also lived in Europe. This crocodile-faced predator had a long snout with straight teeth, large arms with huge claws made for catching fish.

Baryonyx's more famous relative, Spinosaurs, was truly bizarre. Spinosaurus was thought to have been just a large version of Baryonyx with a sail but new finds changed all that.

Not only was Spinosaurus' whole body much longer than previously thought, his hind legs were incredibly short. This means that Spinosaurus was undoubtedly a semi-aquatic dinosaur.

Microraptor was a strange feathered dinosaur from China. Though he had four wings, he could not fly, but rather glided from tree to tree. This would be great for catching insects.

Oviraptor was also a feathered dinosaur. Its name means "Egg Thief" because it was found on top of another dinosaur's eggs, but in fact they were its own nest.

One of the most famous dinosaurs, Velociraptor, was a native of Mongolia. Like its relative, Microraptor, Velociraptor is known to be covered in feathers.

Velociraptor was also about 3 feet tall, about the size of a Turkey. Their favorite food may have been the frilled dinosaur Protoceratops.

Gallimimus lived alongside Velociraptor, but may have been too big for them to catch. Gallimimus resembled an Ostrich very much.

Ornithomimus was Gallimimus' American cousin. Ornithomimus means "Bird Mimic". These dinosaurs had no teeth in their beaks.

Not far away, Pachycephalosaurs were grazing on the Late Cretaceous vegetation of North America. Pachycephalosaurus had a round dome-like cranium that was thought to be used for fighting.

Paleontologists haven't figured out how Pachycephalosaurs fought. Whether ramming like Muck Ox or pushing like Warthogs, they must have been used for more than showing off.

Hadrosaurs were the most common type of dinosaur in the late Cretaceous. They came in so many different head shapes and crest displays.

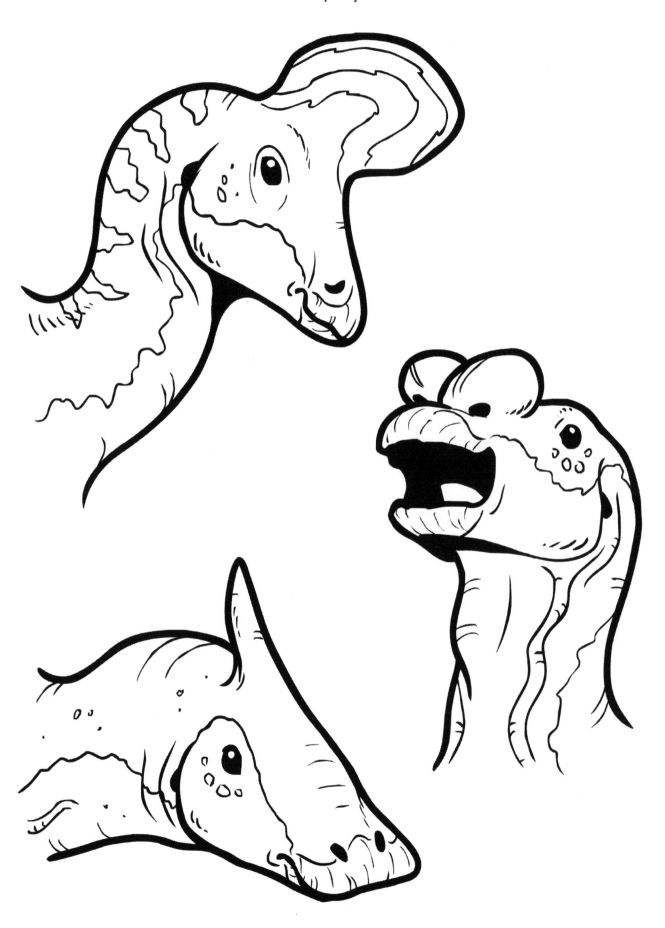

One of most famous was Parasaurolophus. Parasaurolophus used it's hollow, channeled crest to make trumpeting sounds just like a trombone.

The most common duckbill of the late Cretaceous in North America was the Edmontosaurus. With jaws that packed over 1,000 teeth, Edmontosaurus ate a tremendous amount of plants.

Smaller herbivores like Thescelosaurus also lived on the forested floodplains of prehistoric Montana. Like small antelope, always on the move for food.

The most heavily armored dinosaurs lived at this time. Ankylosaurus was like a vegetable-eating tank. If his armor wasn't enough, he also had a club on the end of his tail.

This tail was capable of breaking bone and could have been used to not only fight rival Ankylosaurus, but to fend off carnivores as well.

The most unique dinosaur family must have been the ceratopsians. This is the family of horned dinosaurs like Diabloceratops and Nasutuceratops.

Like the hadrosaurs, their heads came in such weird and unique varieties. Some were wacky like Styracosaurus and Kosmoceratops.

Of course our favorite of them all was the great, majestic Triceratops!
This three-horned giant was the biggest of all the ceratopsians.

Its horns and frill may have been used for showing off and fighting other Triceratops. We now know that ceratopsians, like Triceratops, may have had quills on their backs.

The late Cretaceous brought about the mightiest predator of the dinosaur age! The mighty Tyrannosaurus Rex. King of the dinosaurs.

T. Rex was a powerful beast, weighing up to 7 tons and was as long as 40 feet. Her bite was the most powerful of any land animal ever, strong enough to crush a car!

Tyrannosaurus was one of the most ferocious of killers on earth, but may have also been the most caring of parents. It's most likely T. Rexes lived in family groups.

Paleontologists think T. Rex most likely had feathers since its ancestors like Guanlong did. Never the less, it was still a fearsome predator.

As powerful as T. Rex was, she was no match for the forces that were about to destroy her world. 66 million years ago, an asteroid 6 miles wide crashed into earth.

This extinction wiped out 60 percent of life on earth. Most of the dinosaurs are now extinct.

All we have left of the greatest creatures to have ever walked the earth now are their fossilized bones.

But not all dinosaurs are gone, for their modern decedents, the birds, are here to remind us of the great and extraordinary that roamed the earth long ago.

Made in the USA
San Bernardino, CA
16 November 2017